AARUSHI'S TEENAGE JOURNEY

SEHAR RASHID

Made with ♥ on the Notion Press Platform
www.notionpress.com

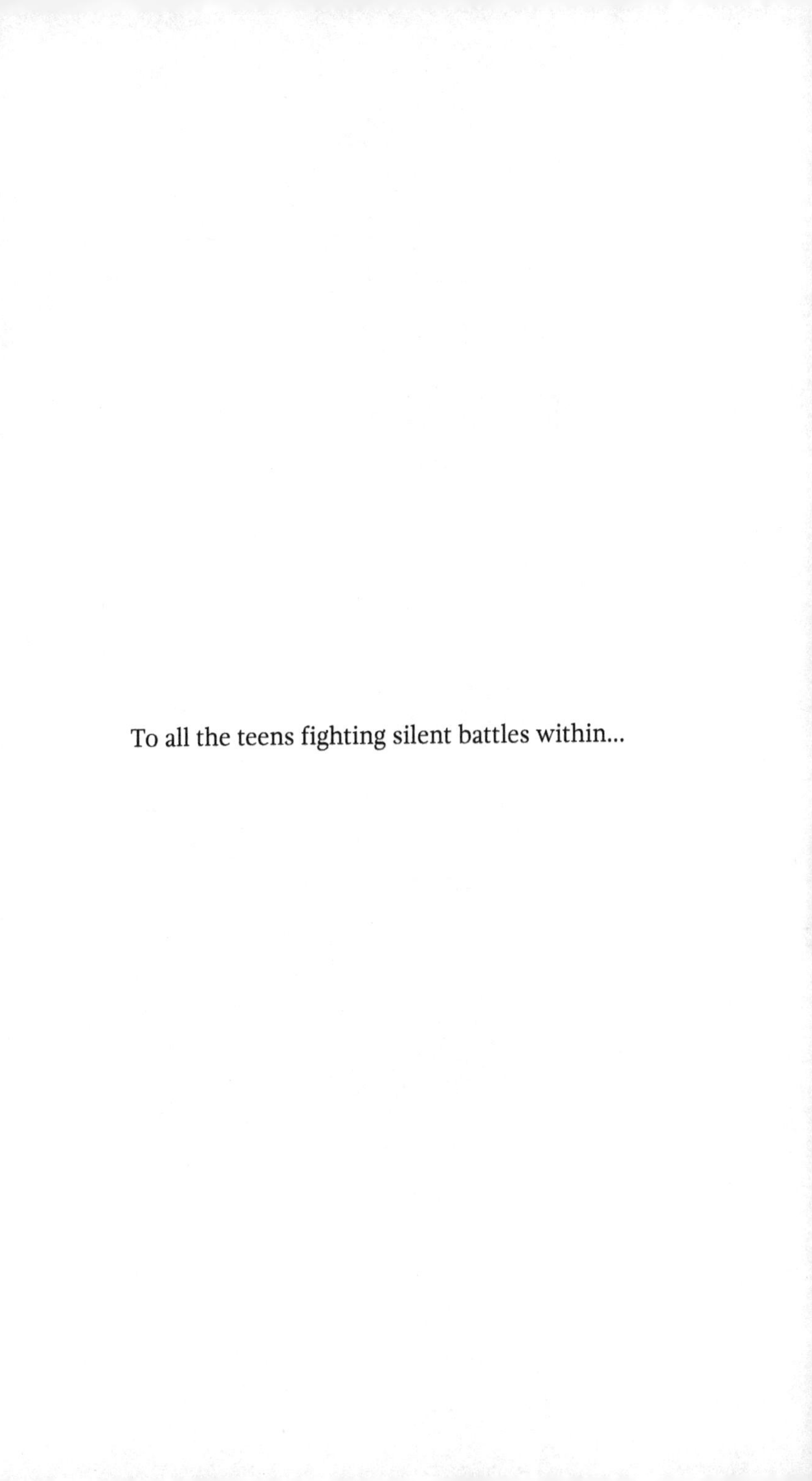

To all the teens fighting silent battles within...

Contents

Preface   *vii*

  1. Meet Aarushi   1

  2. A Friend Which None Can Have   4

  3. Brilliant But Neglected   7

  4. Handwriting Woes   10

  5. Teenage Devil   13

  6. Lonely Aarushi   16

  7. The Fight Begins   19

  8. We Are In This Together   22

  9. Fails To Express   25

10. Aarushi's Condition Got Worse   28

11. The Resolve   31

12. The New Guy In The Class   34

13. Falling For Each Other   36

14. The Unexpected Turn   38

ABOUT THE AUTHOR   41

Preface

A research shows that more than 30 percent of teenagers suffer from teenage stress and very less of them know how to tackle these teenage issues, we as teens face an attraction phase as well but even this is not discussed much in our society. Being a teenager I think that it's time we should discusss these things. This book is born from a desire to shed light upon the shadows that accompany us during this age.

To every teenager who has felt the weight of the world upon their shoulders, know that you are not alone. Remember, after the darkness their is light, a ray of hope, love and endless possibilities.

CHAPTER ONE

MEET AARUSHI

I jumped out of the taxi, my heart racing, and hurried up to Aarushi's house. Panting, I called out, "Hey Aaru!"

She appeared at the door, her eyes sparkling with a mix of excitement and relief. Aarushi, with her gentle, courageous eyes, and a hint of innocence that belied her maturity, looked like she hadn't changed a bit in the month I'd been away.

"Vidhi!" She threw her arms around me. "You finally came! I've been waiting forever. What took you so long?"

We've been best friends since childhood, and our bond feels unbreakable. I'd been out of town with my family for a month, attending a series of events at my Grandpa's house.

"Tell me about it. The traffic here is insane," I said, trying to catch my breath.

"Forget the traffic. Come on in!" Aarushi grabbed my hand and led me to her room.

"I brought your favorite pizza from that place you love," she said, her eyes twinkling with excitement.

"Thank you so much!" I grinned, thrilled at the gesture.

"It's a bit cold now, but let's dig in," she said, giggling. We settled down and enjoyed the pizza, chatting about everything and nothing.

As I was leaving, Aarushi called out, "You're coming to school tomorrow, right?"

"Of course, I'll be there. I'll even bring your notebooks so I can catch up on what I missed."

"I'm so glad you'll finally be back at school," she sighed in relief.

"Wait a minute," I said, suddenly curious. "Were you on your own all this time? You should really try to be a little more open and make some new friends."

"I don't need more friends. You're more than enough for me," she replied, her words as warm and comforting as ever.

I smiled, feeling a mix of gratitude and affection for her. "Okay, I'm heading home now. See you tomorrow!" I said, giving her a quick hug before leaving.

No matter where we are or what we're doing, our conversations are endless. If you were to read our WhatsApp chats, you'd be surprised that the person on the other side is Aarushi. The next day at school, I sat with another girl just to tease her. Aarushi, spotting me, came over and said, "Come sit with me."

"I'm good here," I replied with a grin.

"Fine, stay there if you want," she pouted, then flopped down on her bench, clearly jealous.

A few minutes later, I approached her. "Hey Aaru, can I sit with you now?"

"Why? Do you want to sit with her instead?" she asked, her eyes twinkling with mock irritation.

"Alright, alright," I said, pretending to leave. As I turned, she called out, "Wait, come back!"

I knew she'd change her mind. I loved how adorable she was when she acted like this.

But then, something serious happened. Aarushi got called to the office because her father had phoned, saying her mother had been in an accident and needed her at home urgently.

As she packed up her things, I asked, "What's going on?"

"Mumma had an accident," she said, tears welling up. She usually keeps her emotions in check but couldn't hide them from me.

"Everything will be alright," I said, trying to calm her. "Just go home and drive safely."

She left, her worry for her family evident in her hurried steps. Aarushi is fiercely protective of her family and loves them deeply. Even though they care for her too, she's not particularly close to them. She tends to put others before herself, is kind and cheerful, yet struggles with shyness and confidence in social situations. Despite her introverted nature, she finds joy in small things and is incredibly strong and resilient.

CHAPTER TWO

A FRIEND WHICH NONE CAN HAVE

One evening, we were out with some friends at a restaurant, deciding what to order. Everyone was chatting and throwing out suggestions, but Aarushi remained quiet. This wasn't unusual; she's often reserved around people she doesn't know well.

"Aaru, what do you want to order?" I asked, hoping to get her input.

"I don't know. Just order whatever you like. I'll eat that," she replied with a shrug.

We enjoyed our meal and then headed to a nearby park to hang out. The evening was going great until suddenly, chaos erupted. A group of armed men stormed into the park, causing everyone to panic. People were running in every direction.

In the scramble, I twisted my ankle and couldn't move. Everyone else bolted, leaving me behind, but Aarushi stayed. She ran to me, grabbing my hand. "Come on, get up. We'll go together," she urged.

"Aaru, it's not safe. I can't walk. Just go!" I pleaded.

"I'm not leaving you here alone," she said firmly. Despite the danger, she refused to abandon me.

In that terrifying moment, I realized just how rare and special Aarushi's friendship was. While most people would have fled for their own safety, she stayed behind to help me. She was the kind of friend who would face danger head-on without a second thought.

With great effort, Aarushi helped me stand and guided me behind a large drum for cover. The scene around us was a nightmare—gunshots, screams, and chaos everywhere. I was scared, but Aarushi remained calm and determined.

Finally, we made it to her scooter. Aarushi drove at breakneck speed, her focus and determination clear in her every move. We reached her house, the closest safe place we could find.

She rang the bell and shouted, "Mumma, Papa, open up!"

Her parents, already anxious from hearing the news, rushed to the door. "Aarushi, are you okay?" they asked, their faces etched with worry.

"Yes, Mumma, but Vidhi is hurt. I need to get her to my room," Aarushi said, trying to stay calm.

Once inside, Aarushi helped me into her room and began administering first aid. It wasn't until then that I noticed she was also injured—scratches on her arms and a bleeding leg.

"Aaru, you're hurt too! Let me take care of you," I said, concerned.

Her jeans were stained red from the bleeding near her knee, but she brushed off my worries. I tended to her wounds as best as I could, and then she received a call from my parents. They were frantic but relieved to hear we were safe at Aarushi's house.

Aarushi's parents came over with some medicines and expressed their gratitude for her bravery. They were relieved to hear how she had stayed behind to protect me.

"Aaru, I can't thank you enough. What would I have done without you? I love you," I said, my voice filled with emotion.

"I love you too, idiot. My life would be incomplete without you," Aarushi replied with a smile.

That night, I stayed at Aarushi's house. The city was under curfew for over a week, and I was grateful to have such a true friend by my side.

CHAPTER THREE

BRILLIANT BUT NEGLECTED

Aarushi was an exceptional student. Her academic excellence was well-known, yet she seemed to be overlooked by both her teachers and her own family. Her elder sister, who wasn't as academically inclined, received far more attention, much to Aarushi's silent frustration.

The half-yearly results were just two days away, and anticipation was high. Our teacher came into the classroom and praised several students for their outstanding performance. The classmates were buzzing, expecting Aarushi's name to be called out, but when it wasn't, a heavy silence fell over the room. Aarushi's face fell, and I could see the disappointment in her eyes. She believed she had performed poorly this time, but I reassured her, "Don't worry, Aarushi. Sir might have just forgotten to mention you. Let's wait for the results."

The results were finally announced, and Aarushi scored an impressive 95 percent. We were overjoyed, celebrating her success as we headed home. But when Aarushi shared her results with her parents, their reaction was anything but celebratory. "What will you do with these marks? The subject you've chosen is useless," they said dismissively.

Aarushi was crushed. She ran to her room, tears streaming down her face. It wasn't just the disappointment in her marks that hurt; it was the lack of recognition and support from her family.

To understand why her parents reacted this way, we need to look back at Aarushi's childhood. When Aarushi was in 1st grade, she worked diligently, motivated by the constant scolding her elder sister received for not studying enough. While her sister received help with her homework from their mother, Aarushi did all her work independently, hoping that by being perfect, she'd earn the same attention.

But despite her hard work and punctuality, Aarushi never received more than a cursory acknowledgment. "Aarushi is a good girl; she completes all her work," her parents would say. They never fully grasped the depth of her efforts or her desire for genuine recognition.

There were many nights when Aarushi would cry herself to sleep after receiving good results, feeling that her achievements were overshadowed by her sister's shortcomings. Despite her maturity and accomplishments, she was often left feeling neglected.

One memorable moment from her early years was when she proudly showed her 1st-grade results to her mother. "Mumma, look, I got 95 percent!" she said, her eyes sparkling with excitement. Her elder sister's results, at 60 percent, were met with a different response.

"Vidushi, you need to work harder. I'll help you," their mother said.

"Very good, Aarushi," was all she got in response.

Aarushi longed for the same kind of encouragement from her mother, but it was never forthcoming. She felt that her maturity had unintentionally isolated her from the attention she craved. "Had I not been so mature, I might have received the attention I wanted," she often reflected.

In her eyes, you could see a deep pain, a loneliness that had become a part of her. She had learned to make solitude her companion, hiding her longing for attention behind a facade of self-sufficiency. Despite her accomplishments and maturity, she remained a special, misunderstood soul.

Aarushi's story is a poignant reminder of how even those who seem to have everything together can struggle with feelings of neglect and isolation. Her journey illustrates the importance of recognizing and valuing each individual's efforts and emotions, regardless of their outward maturity.

CHAPTER FOUR

HANDWRITING WOES

When we think of a "good student," we often imagine someone with neat handwriting. But Aarushi didn't fit this image. Her handwriting was messy, like a child's scrawl, and despite her best efforts, she couldn't seem to improve it. Her brilliance in academics was overshadowed by this one persistent flaw.

I remember the day a new teacher joined our class. His first impression of Aarushi's handwriting was anything but positive. He looked at her notes and, without hesitation, reprimanded her. "I don't expect much from students like you," he said harshly. "Look at your handwriting. It's such a mess. How can I expect you to focus on your studies?"

Aarushi stood there, silent and hurt. When the teacher left, she buried her face in her desk and began to cry. I noticed and went over to her. "Aaru, what's wrong? Are you still upset about that teacher?"

"No, it's nothing. I just have a headache," she mumbled, not lifting her head.

"Really? Show me your face then," I insisted.

She lifted her head, revealing red eyes and no tears. "You were crying, weren't you?" I asked gently.

"No, I wasn't crying. I really have a terrible headache," she insisted, though I could tell something was off.

We went home, and Aarushi locked herself in her room. I could sense she was upset, but I didn't know how deeply. Later that evening, while she was working on school assignments, her mother came across her notebook.

"You don't know how to hold a pen properly," her mother said, scrutinizing the messy handwriting. "Look at this. It's like a child's writing. How can anyone believe you're in class 10? And look at your sister's writing—so neat and beautiful. Why can't you write like that?"

Aarushi's shoulders slumped. "Mumma, I try, but I just can't improve," she said quietly.

"Those are just excuses," her mother retorted.

Her mother's words cut deep. Aarushi had faced this criticism for years, and it had left her feeling ashamed of her handwriting. She was embarrassed to write in front of others, hiding her notes and avoiding writing tasks whenever possible.

"I wish I could improve my writing," Aarushi confided to me later. "Then maybe I wouldn't feel so embarrassed or ashamed. I don't understand why, even after all my daily practice, it never gets better."

"It's totally fine, Aarushi. Your handwriting doesn't define you. You're amazing just the way you are," I said, trying to comfort her.

She smiled faintly send replied, "It's easy to say those words, but putting them into practice is much harder."

Despite her struggles, Aarushi's strength and determination shone through. She managed to excel academically, even with the challenges her handwriting posed. Her ability to overcome these obstacles is a testament to her resilience and inner strength.

CHAPTER FIVE

TEENAGE DEVIL

For Aarushi, the age of 16 was a turning point. It wasn't just about school or friends; it was a whirlwind of peer pressure, mounting responsibilities, and a deep-seated loneliness. She struggled under the weight of expectations, and her strained relationship with her parents only made things worse.

One evening, as Aarushi sat in her room, her mother walked in and scolded her. "Why are you always on your phone? You should be doing something productive. Every time I see you, you're glued to that screen."

It was a comment many teenagers hear from their parents, but for Aarushi that day, it was the last straw. After her mother left, Aarushi's frustration boiled over. She started throwing things around her room, her anger spilling out uncontrollably. And then, in a moment of raw vulnerability, she broke down, her tears mingling with the mess she had made.

She was also snapping at the smallest things. I remember one day, I accidentally dropped a book from the desk. Aarushi's reaction was extreme. "Why do you always drop books? You know I hate it when books fall, yet you keep doing it!" she snapped.

"Aaru, it fell by mistake. I won't make it happen again," I said, trying to stay calm.

"You... just..." She trailed off, her frustration evident. Her head hung low, and I could see the strain etched on her face.

"Aaru, what's going on? I'm really sorry," I said, trying to console her.

"No, it's my fault. I'm sorry for being so rude," she replied, her voice cracking.

That moment made me realize that something was deeply troubling Aarushi. The cheerful, lively friend I knew was slipping away, replaced by someone who was on edge and easily upset. It was clear she was struggling, though she didn't openly talk about it.

But amidst the turmoil, there were moments of unexpected joy. One day, I handed her a chocolate, and her face lit up with a happiness that seemed so genuine, yet fleeting. She was like a child finding solace in a small treat, if only for a moment.

We spent an afternoon in her room, laughing at silly jokes. Suddenly, tears welled up in her eyes. "Hey, are you crying?" I asked, concerned.

"No, I think there's something in my eye," she said quickly, trying to brush it off.

I wasn't convinced but didn't push further. She changed the subject with another joke, trying to mask her emotions with humor.

Aarushi's mood swings became more frequent. One moment she'd be laughing, the next, she'd be in tears. Her anger seemed to come out of nowhere, and her breakdowns were intense. It was as though she was battling a storm inside her, but no one, not even her parents or me, could understand what was happening.

Slowly but surely, Aarushi was sinking into a state of depression. The girl who used to bring joy to everyone around her was now struggling silently with her own pain. Her stress was escalating, becoming a heavy burden that she carried alone.

For many teenagers, like Aarushi, the pressures of school, family, and social life can become overwhelming. They might feel isolated, even when surrounded by people. It's crucial to recognize these signs and understand that it's okay to seek help. No one should face such struggles alone, and reaching out to friends, family, or professionals can make a significant difference.

CHAPTER SIX

LONELY AARUSHI

Aarushi's insecurities had begun to consume her. She found herself lost in thoughts, questioning everything. "What if my friendship ends? What if my best friend leaves me? What if my parents don't understand me and don't let me follow my dreams? Everything will be shattered. What if..."

The next day, a small argument between her parents set her off. The tension in the house was palpable. Aarushi, already on edge, couldn't handle it. She retreated to her room, her emotions boiling over. Her anger erupted into loud, frustrated shouts, drawing the attention of her parents.

"What is this behavior, Aarushi?" her mother's voice cut through the air.

"Why are you becoming so senseless and stupid?" her father added harshly.

The stress of the argument with her parents spilled over into a confrontation with me later that day. We fought over something trivial, but to Aarushi, it felt like another betrayal in a world that seemed to be falling apart.

That night, alone in her room, Aarushi sat at her desk, scribbling furiously on a piece of paper. Her words were a raw reflection of her turmoil:

"I don't know what's happening in my life. Everything feels shattered—my family, my friend, everything. No one understands me. Everything is slipping out of my hands, and it's getting worse. I can't stand this anymore. I'm sorry to my life, but I want to end this pain. I can't handle the taunts from anyone. It's over. I was never so weak to do this, but now I don't have any other choice. I tried so hard, but now I'm done."

With the letter finished, Aarushi's next step was terrifying. She ran to the kitchen, grabbed a knife, and pressed it against her wrist, desperate to end her suffering. But just then, her hand brushed against a hot pot, jolting her back to reality. The searing pain from the pot made her drop the knife in shock.

"What was I going to do?" she whispered to herself, her voice trembling. "How could I be so cowardly?"

Aarushi was fortunate that the incident with the pot had brought her back from the brink. Not everyone has such a moment of clarity. She returned to her room, her anger turning into a storm of tears. She threw her clothes and bedding around in frustration, creating chaos in her sanctuary. She collapsed onto the floor, clutching a pillow to her chest as she cried with all her might.

The people around her couldn't see the depth of her pain, and I only learned of her struggles later when I discovered that heartbreaking letter in her room. Aarushi later reflected on the incident, saying, "I was stupid, but that pot was a lucky charm that helped me regain my senses in time."

Back in her room that night, Aarushi took a deep breath. She folded the letter, hiding it behind her desk. She spoke to herself, her voice steady despite the tears, "I know things are very hard, but I'm not that weak. I might feel alone, but

I'll fight and win. I don't know what the future holds, but I'm not giving up."

She cried herself to sleep, a mix of hopelessness and resolve in her heart. That night marked the beginning of a slow transformation. Aarushi was still broken, still hurting, but a fierce determination began to grow within her. It wasn't an immediate change, but a gradual process of finding her inner strength and courage.

To understand how Aarushi emerged from the darkness and began to rebuild her life, keep reading. Her journey was just beginning, and the road to healing would be long and challenging, but it was a path she was determined to walk.

CHAPTER SEVEN

THE FIGHT BEGINS

The morning after Aarushi's breakdown, she woke up with a renewed sense of determination. There was a noticeable change in her demeanor—her smile was back, and she seemed to have found a way to calm herself amidst the chaos she was facing. When we met at school, she approached me with a heartfelt apology.

"Vidhi, I'm really sorry for my behavior lately. I've been so rude," she said.

I was taken aback. "Aaru, it's like the sun came from a different direction today. Are you okay?" I asked, trying to gauge her sincerity.

"Yes, everything is fine," she replied, though her tone was different from before.

"Okay, then," I said, a bit confused but relieved to see her in a better mood.

Throughout the day, Aarushi remained calm and composed, even when I purposely knocked over a book on the floor. Normally, she would have been irritated, but today, she picked it up without a hint of frustration. I tried to push her buttons, asking the same questions repeatedly, but she maintained her cool, which was unusual for her.

Later that evening, I went over to Aarushi's house. She was in her room when I arrived.

"Oh hey, Vidhi!" she greeted me cheerfully.

"Hi, Aaru. I'm starving. Can you get me something to eat?" I asked.

"Sure, wait here," she said, heading to the kitchen.

While she was gone, I started looking around her room. As I moved around, my hand accidentally brushed against something that fell to the floor. I bent down to pick it up and noticed a folded paper behind the desk. Curious, I unfolded it and recognized it as the letter Aarushi had written the previous night. My heart sank as I read it.

When Aarushi returned, I couldn't hold back my concern. I quickly hugged her. "Aaru, I'm so sorry. I didn't know you were going through so much."

She looked confused. "What happened?"

"Look at this," I said, showing her the letter. "How could you keep this from me? You're my best friend. What would I have done if something had happened to you?"

"Nothing happened," she said, trying to brush it off.

"Then why write this letter? Tell me what's really going on," I insisted.

Aarushi hesitated, and I could see the conflict in her eyes. "Everything's okay. I just felt overwhelmed," she said softly.

"Aarushi, if you consider me even a small part of your life, you need to tell me what's going on. Otherwise, I'm leaving," I said firmly.

Her defenses crumbled, and she began to cry. "Okay, fine. Calm down," she said, breaking down.

"Aaru, I'm here for you," I said, trying to comfort her.

"I just want to go somewhere where it's just me. I'm so frustrated with everything. I feel like I'm losing control," she admitted, her voice trembling.

Hearing her talk about her struggles was both shocking and heartbreaking. I had been making light of her mood swings, not realizing the depth of her pain. It became clear that Aarushi was carrying a heavy burden that she had been hiding from everyone, even me.

That night, as Aarushi shared her feelings with me, I understood the importance of being there for someone in their darkest moments. Her vulnerability was a reminder of how crucial it is to communicate and support one another, especially during tough times.

For anyone struggling like Aarushi, remember that it's okay to reach out for help. Sometimes, the simple act of opening up to a friend or loved one can make a world of difference. Don't wait until you're at breaking point—talk to someone who cares about you. You don't have to face your challenges alone.

As Aarushi and I talked that night, it was clear that her journey wasn't over. It would take time and support for her to heal and find her balance. But by breaking the silence and sharing her struggles, she took the first step toward recovery.

CHAPTER EIGHT

WE ARE IN THIS TOGETHER

"I'm sorry you've been through so much, but you always say that suicide isn't the answer. How could you even consider it?" I asked, my concern palpable.

Aarushi sighed. "I don't know what got into me. It was like I lost control for a moment."

"Well, thankfully, you're safe now. Let's focus on solving the problem together," I said, trying to shift our focus to finding solutions.

"Yes, I'm trying," Aarushi replied, her voice tinged with determination.

"We'll face this together," I assured her. "Thanks for being honest with me." I could see the relief in her eyes, and it was clear that sharing her feelings had eased some of her burden.

"Stop getting all emotional now. I'm starving—what did you bring to eat?" I said, trying to lighten the mood.

"Oh right, I brought sandwiches," she said, smiling slightly.

"Great, let's eat," I said, taking the sandwiches from her.

As we ate, I thought about how important it is to share what we're feeling rather than letting our thoughts consume us. Sometimes, just talking to someone who cares can make a huge difference.

Aarushi wanted to keep her struggles private, so we decided to handle it ourselves for now. However, the next morning, Aarushi woke up with a fever and decided to take a leave from school. Her mother repeatedly called her, but she delayed answering and was eventually scolded for not helping around the house.

"Why did you take leave from school if you're not going to help me?" her mother said, frustration evident in her voice.

"I'm sorry, Mumma," Aarushi replied, trying to keep her voice steady.

"Fine, just help me now," her mother said.

As Aarushi helped with the chores, she felt a pang of neglect. Despite her best efforts to hide her tears, they slipped down her cheeks. She took her medicine and rested in the afternoon, but it seemed like no one noticed how sick she was.

Later that evening, Aarushi was plagued with the same insecurities. I texted her to check in, and she shared everything that had happened that day.

"I think they're just busy. If you don't tell them what's going on, how would they know?" I said, trying to offer perspective.

"But I feel like I'm being pushed aside," Aarushi said, her voice heavy with sadness.

"You're overthinking it. The real issue is that you're distant from your parents. If you want them to understand, you need to make an effort to connect with them," I advised.

"But how do I do that when they don't seem to understand me?" Aarushi questioned.

"Start by being open with them. They love you, but they might not know what you're going through because you keep it to yourself. Try to bridge the gap by sharing your feelings and letting them in," I suggested.

"Do you really think that will work?" Aarushi asked, her tone a mix of skepticism and hope.

"Yes, I believe it's worth trying. It's a step towards resolving the misunderstandings," I replied.

Aarushi nodded thoughtfully. "Alright, I'll give it a try."

That evening, Aarushi began to think about how she could approach her parents. It was clear that rebuilding that connection wouldn't be easy, but it was a necessary step for her emotional well-being.

For anyone feeling misunderstood or distant from their loved ones, remember that opening up and making an effort to connect can lead to understanding and support. Don't let insecurities and misunderstandings fester—take the step to bridge the gap and build stronger, more supportive relationships.

Fails to express

Chapter 9: Breaking the Silence

The next day, Aarushi's fever persisted, but she insisted on coming to school. Her exhaustion was evident, and her usually vibrant demeanor was subdued.

"Why did you come to school if you're not feeling well?" I asked, concerned.

"I just want to stay away from home," she replied softly. "I'm not feeling good there."

"Will being here help?" I questioned, hoping to understand her reasoning.

"I'm not running away. I just need some time to clear my mind. I want to escape the negative thoughts for a bit," she explained.

I nodded, understanding her need for a mental break. We spent the day together, and for a few hours, it felt like we were able to put the weight of our worries aside.

However, that evening, things took a turn for the worse. Aarushi made a mistake at home, leading to a scolding from her parents. Their frustration was palpable.

"Aarushi, what happened to you? You used to be so responsible. Now you're acting so strangely and irresponsibly," her mother scolded.

"You should know better. You're educated and should be handling things properly," her father added, his tone sharp.

Aarushi, who usually took their criticism silently, couldn't contain her emotions any longer. The weight of everything she had been holding inside came crashing out.

"I'm tired of all this," she burst out. "I've been suffering from a fever since yesterday, and did anyone notice? I know you love me, but it doesn't feel that way. I keep quiet because I don't want to hurt you, but all these criticisms are hurting me. I've tried so hard to be responsible, to meet your expectations, but it's only brought me pain. I want to have a close relationship with you, like my sister has. But I feel like everything is slipping through my fingers."

Her parents were taken aback, their faces showing shock and concern. They hadn't realized the depth of her struggle and the emotional toll it had taken on her.

Aarushi, overwhelmed by her emotions, ran to her room. Her parents, deeply affected by her outburst, discussed the situation privately. After some time, her mother came to her room with a different approach.

"Aarushi, take these medicines," her mother said gently, handing her the medication.

Aarushi took the medicine and fell asleep, exhausted from the emotional release. The next morning, she woke up to find her parents still upset.

"What happened?" Aarushi asked, her voice filled with confusion.

"You need to learn how to speak to your elders," her mother said, her tone still tinged with frustration. "If you were unwell, you should have told us instead of making it into such a big issue."

"I'm sorry, Mumma," Aarushi said, her heart sinking. She felt misunderstood and hurt by the ongoing tension.

Her mother's reaction left Aarushi feeling disheartened. Despite her attempt to express her feelings, it seemed that her parents were still focused on the way she communicated her distress rather than addressing her emotional needs.

Sometimes things go haywire, and we are misunderstood by parents, and trust me that's completely okay. It happens many times that we fail to express ourselves properly but if we try to keep calm and make them understand our situation, it will help us to solve our problems.

For teenagers facing similar issues, remember that expressing your feelings honestly is crucial, even when it feels difficult. It's important to approach these conversations with a focus on finding mutual understanding and solutions, rather than letting misunderstandings and frustrations build up.

AARUSHI'S CONDITION GOT WORSE

Chapter 10: Unspoken Pain

Aarushi was devastated after her outburst and felt deeply regretful for the confrontation with her parents. She called her elder sister, trying to maintain a semblance of normalcy.

"How are you, Di?" Aarushi asked, her voice faltering slightly.

"I'm good. How come you're calling me?" her sister replied with a hint of surprise.

"Just wanted to check in. How's everything going at the hostel?" Aarushi tried to sound casual.

"Everything's fine here, Aaru. How about you?" her sister asked, sensing something was off.

Their conversation flowed into everyday topics, but Aarushi struggled to mention her recent turmoil. After they hung up, Aarushi was left alone with her thoughts, her sadness intensifying.

Later that evening, as she was studying in her room, she heard muffled voices coming from downstairs. Curious and concerned, she ventured down and was horrified to discover her parents in the midst of a heated argument.

"I'll get separated from you!" her father's voice thundered.

"Even I want the same. How can I be with you?" her mother's voice was filled with anguish.

Aarushi's heart sank. The sight of her parents fighting was unbearable. Her mind raced with fear and confusion. She screamed, "Please don't say that, Mumma, Papa! Why are you fighting?"

Her parents, lost in their argument, didn't initially hear her. Aarushi's pleas grew louder, but they were drowned out by their escalating voices. Overwhelmed and distressed, Aarushi's legs gave way, and she collapsed on the floor. Her vision blurred, and she lost consciousness.

Her parents, finally noticing her, rushed to her side. Panic set in as they contacted a doctor, and Aarushi was quickly admitted to the hospital. I heard the news and rushed to the hospital, my heart heavy with worry.

At the hospital, the doctor delivered unsettling news. "It's unusual for someone so young to experience a sudden drop in blood pressure like this. Aarushi is under significant stress, which seems to have overwhelmed her. She'll recover soon, but I strongly advise seeking a psychologist's help. It's crucial to understand and address her mental health to prevent further issues."

Her father's face was a mask of sorrow. "We'll do whatever it takes," he said, his voice filled with regret and concern.

I entered Aarushi's hospital room, finding her lying unconscious. The sight of her so vulnerable and still was heartbreaking. Tears streamed down my face as I spoke softly, "Aaru, why do you suffer so much for everyone? You're so important to me. Please, don't let this pain define you."

Her parents approached, their expressions a mixture of worry and confusion. "Vidhi, did you know about Aarushi's struggles? Why didn't you tell us? What's going on?" they asked urgently.

I stood there, my emotions tangled in a web of guilt and sadness. I had seen the signs but didn't know how to reach out. Now, faced with the reality of her condition, I struggled to find the words.

"I...I didn't know how to tell you," I began, my voice trembling. "Aarushi has been dealing with so much stress, and she's been struggling with her emotions. I saw her hurting but didn't understand how to help her, and I didn't want to overstep."

Aarushi's parents listened intently, their faces reflecting a mix of realization and remorse. The weight of their daughter's silent suffering began to sink in, and they understood that their approach needed to change.

As they absorbed the gravity of the situation, they committed to seeking professional help and mending their relationship with Aarushi. The road ahead would be challenging, but this moment marked the beginning of a critical transformation in their family dynamics.

For teens experiencing similar feelings, it's crucial to communicate openly with those around you and seek help when needed. For families, understanding and support are vital in nurturing emotional well-being and fostering a supportive environment.

CHAPTER ELEVEN

THE RESOLVE

As Aarushi lay in her hospital bed, recovering from her sudden health scare, I felt a profound mix of relief and sorrow. I had been with her through the darkest parts of her journey, and seeing her in such a fragile state was heart-wrenching. Her parents had finally been made aware of the full extent of her struggles, thanks to the psychologist's visit and the revelations I had shared with them. It was a moment of truth that could change everything for Aarushi.

The psychologist, a calm and compassionate figure, spoke with Aarushi for a while. As he concluded his session, he turned to her parents and me.

"After our discussion," the psychologist began, "it's clear that Aarushi is experiencing a significant amount of stress, which is common among teenagers. Over 30% of teens face similar challenges."

Her mother, still shaken, interjected, "But the doctor said that her sudden drop in blood pressure was unusual for someone her age."

"Yes, it is," the psychologist agreed. "It's a serious symptom, but it's crucial to understand that stress and anxiety can manifest in many ways. Although it was recognized late, there's still time to address it. The key is to create a supportive environment for Aarushi. Avoid placing additional pressure on her, and be mindful of your words and actions. Gentle handling during her mood swings and showing understanding will be vital. A lack of attention can lead to deeper depression."

"Thank you, doctor," Aarushi's father said, his voice filled with determination. He escorted the psychologist to the door, a promise of change in his steps.

Returning to Aarushi's room, I found her sleeping peacefully. Her parents sat beside her, their expressions a blend of guilt and hope. When Aarushi awoke, her first sight was her parents, a comforting presence in her recovery.

"Mumma, Papa, what happened?" she asked groggily.

Her mother gently replied, "Nothing, dear. We're so sorry for not understanding you sooner."

Aarushi shook her head, "No, there's nothing like that."

Her father, with a warm smile, offered her a plate of her favorite snacks. "Oh, my little daughter, don't you want these?"

Aarushi's face lit up with joy. "Thanks, Papa!" she said, her eyes sparkling.

"We love you, dear," her mother said, her voice tender.

"I love you too, Mumma, Papa," Aarushi replied, hugging them tightly.

In that embrace, Aarushi felt a profound sense of relief and love. It was as if, in that moment, she had the whole world in her arms. The healing had begun.

Her parents' decision to support her, to truly listen and understand her struggles, marked a significant turning point. The family's journey toward healing was just beginning, but this was a crucial step towards a healthier, more compassionate environment for Aarushi.

Aarushi later reflected on this pivotal moment. "When I hugged them, I felt like I had finally found a place where I truly belonged. It was a victory, not just for me, but for us as a family."

CHAPTER TWELVE

THE NEW GUY IN THE CLASS

Aarushi's stress issues were resolved, but, of course, teenage life never stays quiet for long. In the middle of our 12th year, something unexpected happened—a new student joined our class, which was unusual because no one transfers in mid-year. The teacher announced, "Good morning, students. This is Yash. He's transferred from another branch of our school. Yash, you can take any help from Aarushi, who is the topper of our class. Go ahead and take a seat."

The whole class turned to look at Yash. He was so striking that it was hard to ignore him. During recess, when we were gathered with some classmates, he approached us and asked, "Can I sit with you guys?"

"Yeah, sure," we all agreed, and he took the seat next to Aarushi.

"So, Yash, why the sudden transfer in the middle of the year?" I asked.

"Actually, my father got transferred to this city, so here I am," he explained. "By the way, what's your name?"

"Vidhi," I replied, pointing to Aarushi. "And this is Aarushi."

"Oh, right. The teacher already mentioned her," Yash said, with a grin.

"Yeah, I totally forgot about that," I admitted.

Our conversation continued, but Aarushi mostly listened, not participating much.

The next class was Accountancy, and Yash was clearly struggling with the entries. He kept asking questions but couldn't quite grasp the concepts. The teacher, looking frustrated, said, "Yash, you should get help from one of your classmates, as I suggested."

"Okay, sir," Yash replied, in a drawn-out tone that made the whole class chuckle.

During the free period that followed, Yash came over to our table. "Aarushi, could you help me with these entries?"

"Sure, why not?" Aarushi agreed.

"But Aaru, we were planning to play a game during this time," I reminded her.

"Vidhi, the teacher asked me to help him. What if he fails?" Aarushi said, her tone earnest.

"Are you sure?" I asked, a bit surprised by her dedication.

"Of course. If I don't help him, I'll get in trouble with the teacher," she explained.

"Okay, then I'll go join the others. You can enjoy studying," I said, and left.

As I walked away, I could see that Aarushi was fully committed to helping Yash, even if it meant missing out on some fun.

CHAPTER THIRTEEN

FALLING FOR EACH OTHER

Aarushi began teaching Yash the entries, guiding him patiently. "Here, this is how it's done," she explained, demonstrating the process.

"Thank you, Aarushi. You're such a great teacher," Yash said, genuinely appreciative.

"Let me see your notes," Aarushi requested. "I'll jot down these important points for you."

"Actually, I didn't make any notes for this chapter. I missed some topics because of the shift," Yash admitted.

"Oh, I see," Aarushi said.

"Could you lend me your notebook? I'll complete everything by tomorrow and return it to you," Yash proposed.

"Sure, take it," Aarushi agreed, and then she joined us.

Since their first meeting, Aarushi had felt a growing attraction towards Yash. Over the past month, their bond had strengthened as Yash frequently sought Aarushi's help and they had become close friends.

One evening, Aarushi and I were sitting on the roof, enjoying the cool breeze.

"So, what do you think about Yash?" I asked, curious.

"What...what?" Aarushi hesitated, clearly caught off guard.

"I mean, what type of person is he?" I pressed.

"Oh, he's a good person," Aarushi replied, trying to sound casual.

"And I can tell there's something you're not sharing with me. Spill it," I urged.

"There's nothing to share," Aarushi said, looking away.

"Come on, Aaru, you've started liking him, haven't you?" I teased.

"No... Oh... Actually, yes, or maybe," she admitted, blushing.

"Great, so he's going to be my brother-in-law soon. Wow," I joked sarcastically.

"Are you crazy?" she laughed, playfully swatting at me.

"Okay, okay, sorry. But let me tell you something interesting. According to my sources, he likes you too."

"And who told you that?" she asked, puzzled.

"My sixth sense," I said dramatically. "Have you ever noticed? He admires you, praises you, and looks at you so lovingly."

"Really? The one who's always nonsense is talking about sixth sense?" she laughed.

"Oh, please. You underestimate me way too much. I bet one day he's going to tell you he likes you," I challenged.

"Okay, fine. We'll see," Aarushi replied with a smile, accepting the challenge.

As we continued our conversation, Aarushi seemed more relaxed, and I couldn't help but feel excited about the unfolding drama. Little did we know that this was just the beginning of a new chapter in our lives.

CHAPTER FOURTEEN

THE UNEXPECTED TURN

The next day at school, Yash approached Aarushi with a serious expression. "Aarushi, I want to meet you after school in the ground. Please come, I'll be waiting for you," he said before walking away.

Aarushi shared this with me, and I couldn't hide my excitement. "I told you he's going to propose!"

"It could be anything," Aarushi said, changing the subject.

After school, we headed to the ground where Yash was waiting. As he saw us approaching, he seemed nervous. "I don't know how to say this, actually..." he began, hesitating.

"What's up?" Aarushi asked, looking concerned. I stayed quiet, intrigued by the unfolding scene.

"Look, Aarushi, since I've met you, I've felt a strong connection. The truth is, I think we're more than just friends. I've started liking you," Yash confessed.

Aarushi was taken aback. She grabbed my hand and started walking away. Yash called out to us, "What's wrong, Aarushi? Don't be upset. It's up to you. Take your time to think about it."

"Yash... I'll talk to you later. Bye," Aarushi said, and we left for home.

On the way, I asked her, "You like him too, so why didn't you say yes? You don't seem happy. What's going on?"

"I don't know. I'm happy, but I also feel strange. I don't feel completely good about it," she admitted.

"It's probably just that you're overthinking it. Look, my house is here. Bye, take care," I said.

"Bye," Aarushi replied.

Back at home, Aarushi sat in her room, smiling at the thought of Yash. Suddenly, her mother called her downstairs for snacks as there were guests at the house. Aarushi went to get the snacks, and as she returned, she overheard the guests talking.

"Nowadays, girls are so delicate. They get involved with boys at such a young age. You should keep an eye on Aarushi," one guest said.

Aarushi paused to listen, feeling anxious. Her mother responded, "No, our Aarushi is a mature girl. We trust her."

Aarushi felt a wave of relief and happiness. After giving the snacks, she went back to her room and texted Yash, "Hey Yash, I'm sorry for leaving abruptly."

"It's okay," Yash replied.

"Actually, I think I like you too, but maybe this is just an illusion," Aarushi typed.

"What do you mean?" Yash asked.

"We're both students, and attraction is common at our age. Maybe we're just experiencing that. We need to accept it."

"Yeah, maybe you're right, but..."

"I understand what you're saying and I respect your feelings. However, we must remember not to break our parents' trust. They wouldn't accept us doing anything like this at our age."

"Aarushi, once again, I'm impressed by you. You're very mature. After putting everything aside, can we still be friends like before?" Yash asked.

"Of course, we're still friends," Aarushi replied.

The next day, when I saw both of them, they seemed as usual. I asked Aarushi, "Did you expect his proposal?"

"Look at this," she said, handing me her phone with the chat open. I read through the conversation and was shocked.

"You proved that you're a true friend," I said, hugging her. "You really are a gem, Aarushi."

She smiled, and we laughed together. Despite the ups and downs of teenage life, Aarushi had faced many challenges and emerged stronger. "Actually, I was really attracted to Yash, and resisting those feelings was tough. But with the trust and support of your parents, you can overcome any problem," she said.

Today, Aarushi is 22 years old, a successful entrepreneur, and a college student, while Yash remains a good friend. Aarushi's journey through her teenage years was filled with challenges, but she overcame them all and grew into the successful young woman she is today.

About The Author

Sehar Rashid is a person who has an immense love for writing, she published her debut book in Oct 2021 titled The World of Worlds'. Apart from this she also participated in a national-level poetry contest and got selected among the top 100 youngest poets of India. She believes that writing is not just a hobby but it is one's passion. She wrote Aarushi's Teenage journey at the age of 17.

Connect on Instagram: @author_sehar.rashid

9 798886 676907